by
Luis

Luis

LINDSAY BARRETT GEORGE

My Bunny and Me

GREENWILLOW BOOKS
A IMPRINT OF HARPERCOLLINSPUBLISHERS

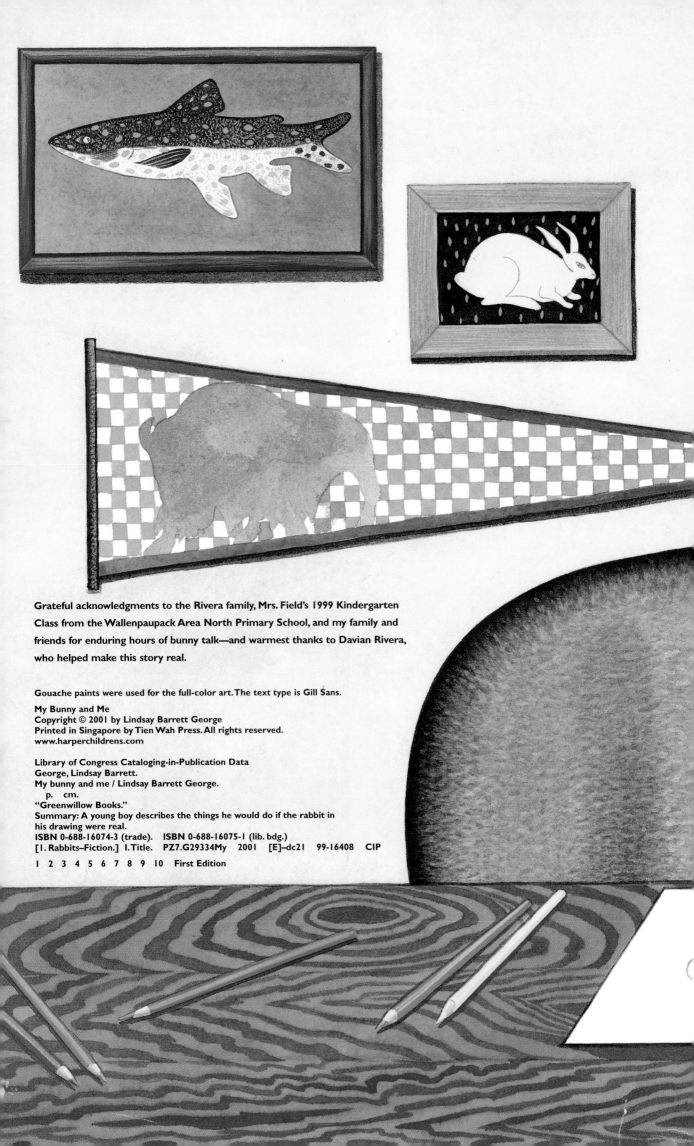

Grateful acknowledgments to the Rivera family, Mrs. Field's 1999 Kindergarten
Class from the Wallenpaupack Area North Primary School, and my family and
friends for enduring hours of bunny talk—and warmest thanks to Davian Rivera,
who helped make this story real.

Gouache paints were used for the full-color art. The text type is Gill Sans.

Library of Congress Cataloging-in-Publication Data
George, Lindsay Barrett.
My bunny and me / Lindsay Barrett George.
    p.   cm.
"Greenwillow Books."
Summary: A young boy describes the things he would do if the rabbit in
his drawing were real.
ISBN 0-688-16074-3 (trade).   ISBN 0-688-16075-1 (lib. bdg.)
[1. Rabbits–Fiction.] I. Title. PZ7.G29334My 2001 [E]–dc21 99-16408 CIP

1 2 3 4 5 6 7 8 9 10   First Edition

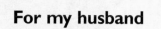

For my husband

If you were real, we could do

lots of things together.

We could stand
in a puddle

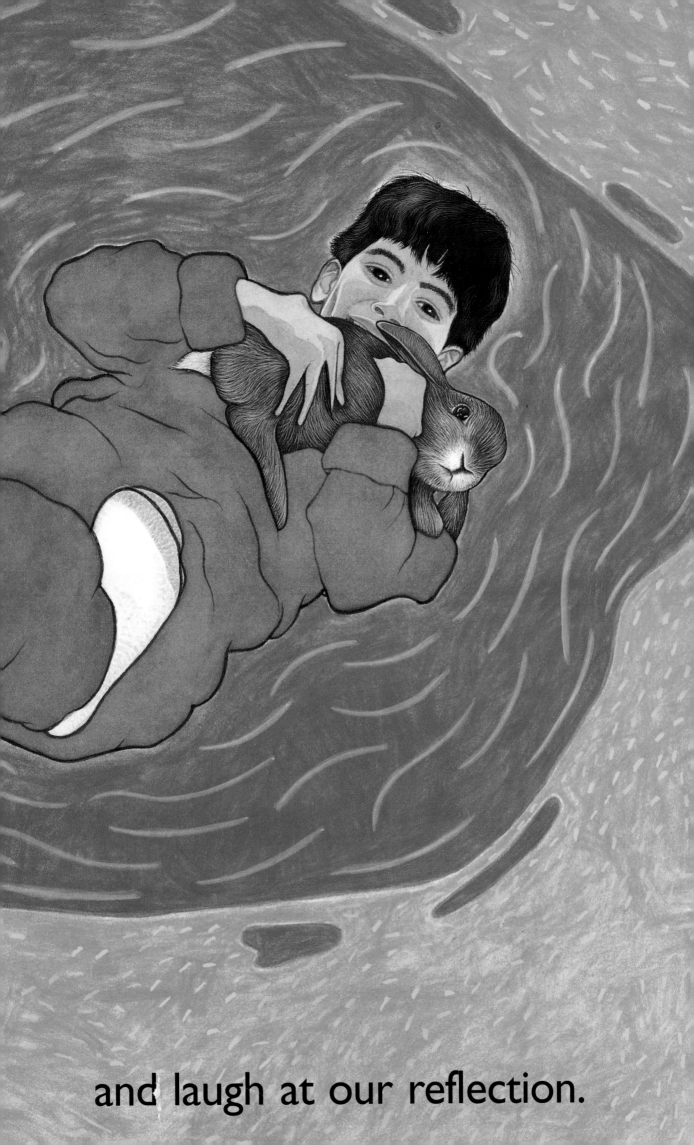

and laugh at our reflection.

You could dig a burrow,

and I would line it with grass.

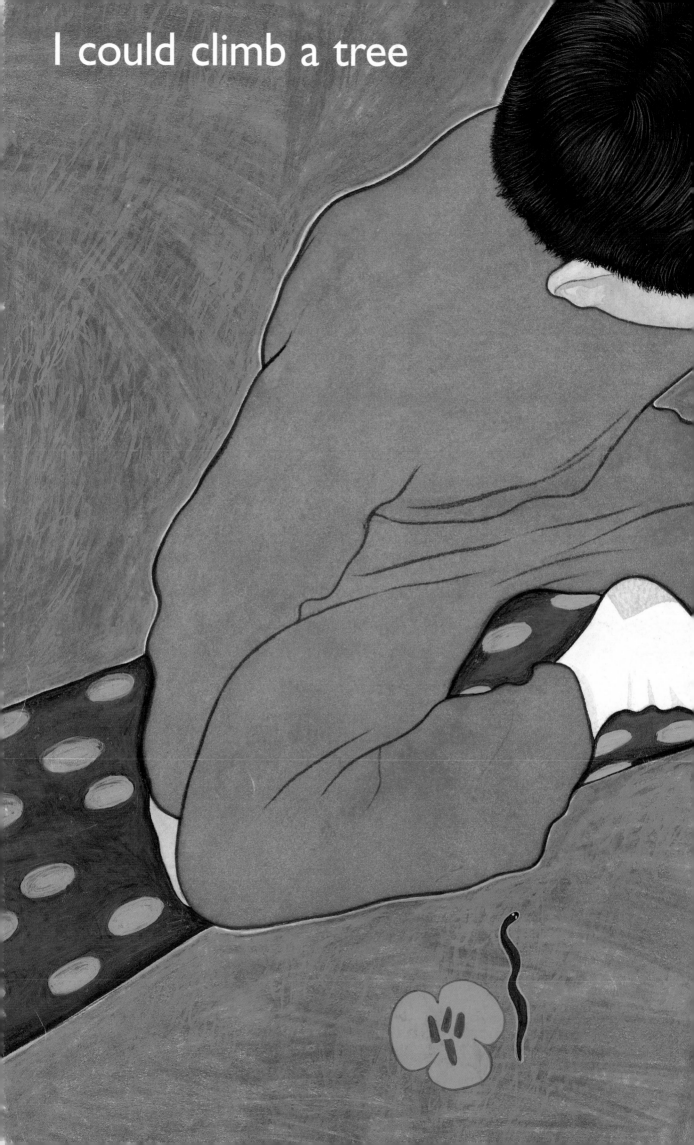

I could climb a tree

and look down
at you.

You
could hide
in my yard,

and I would
find you.

I could open a book

and read you a story.

We could look out my window

and find the Big Dipper.

And when you were tired,

I would hold you close.

But if you were really real,
what I would do

is let you go.

by
LUIS